ZIG ZAG

Dinosaur Planet

First published 2004
Evans Brothers Limited
2A Portman Mansions
Chiltern St
London WIU 6NR

British Library Cataloguing in Publication Data

Orme, David
    Dinosaurs planet. - (Zig zags)
    1. Dinosaurs - Juvenile fiction 2. Children's stories
    I. Title
    823. 9'14 [J]

ISBN 0237527936

Printed in China by WKT Company Limited

Series Editor: Louise John
Design: Robert Walster
Production: Jenny Mulvanny
Series Consultant: Gill Matthews

ZIG ZAG

Dinosaur Planet

by David Orme

illustrated by Fabiano Fiorin

Evans

Tom and Tammy were space explorers.

One day they came across a new planet.

Tom and Tammy decided
to explore.

"Look!" shouted Tom. "There are dinosaurs everywhere!"

They saw big, slow,
plant-eating dinosaurs.

They saw small, fast,
meat-eating dinosaurs.

Some dinosaurs had horns on their heads.

13

Some dinosaurs had plates on their backs.

15

In the sky, there were flying dinosaurs.

17

In the lake, there were swimming dinosaurs.

18

In the forest, Tom and Tammy found a dinosaur's nest. The babies were just hatching.

"They're very friendly!"
laughed Tammy.

Just then the dinosaurs' mum arrived.

"I don't think she's very friendly!" said Tom.

23

"Quick! Run!" said Tammy.

"Let's get out of here," said
Tom. "What a dangerous
planet!"

25

Tom and Tammy ran back to their space ship.

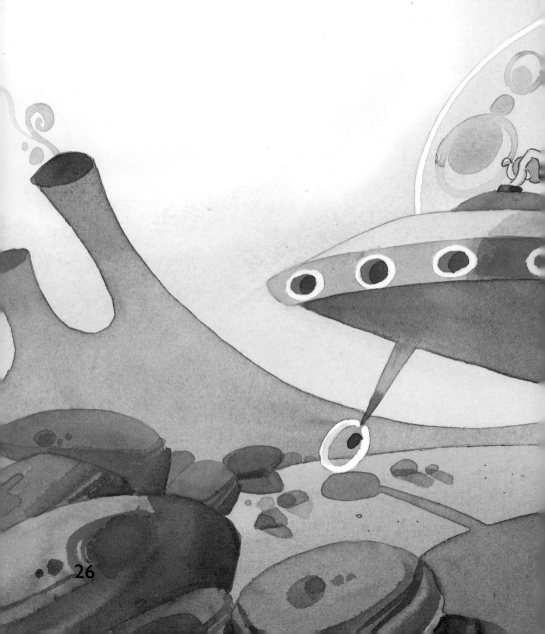

Happy landing!

29

"Oh no! What's that?"
shouted Tom.

"Help!" laughed Tammy.

Why not try reading another ZigZag book?

Dinosaur Planet   ISBN: 0 237 52667 0
by David Orme and Fabiano Fiorin

Tall Tilly   ISBN: 0 237 52668 9
by Jillian Powell and Tim Archbold

Batty Betty's Spells   ISBN: 0 237 52669 7
by Hilary Robinson and Belinda Worsley

The Thirsty Moose   ISBN: 0 237 52666 2
by David Orme and Mike Gordon

The Clumsy Cow   ISBN: 0 237 52656 5
by Julia Moffatt and Lisa Williams

Open Wide!   ISBN: 0 237 52657 3
by Julia Moffatt and Anni Axworthy